To William Cawthra IV   Love, W.C.

NOTE TO PARENTS

Based on the beloved Walt Disney motion picture *Dumbo,* this book focuses on what happens when Dumbo the baby elephant becomes the laughingstock of the circus. His big ears get in his way whenever he tries to join in with the other elephants. At last, only his friend Timothy Mouse still believes Dumbo can be a star.

When Dumbo and Timothy awaken one morning in a treetop, they know something unusual has happened—Dumbo must have flown! Dumbo doesn't believe he can fly until a friendly crow gives him a "magic" feather. With something to hold on to, Dumbo believes. Back at the circus, his new talent astounds everyone until the magic feather slips from his trunk and he begins to fall. It's then that he learns what Timothy has known all along: He can do anything—even fly!—if he only believes he can.

This book recounts one memorable episode from the movie that will help children learn an important lesson about the value of confidence. For the complete story of *Walt Disney's Dumbo,* look for these other Golden Books:

10076   WALT DISNEY's DUMBO
(A Golden Super Shape Book™)

104-53   WALT DISNEY's DUMBO
(A Little Golden Book®)

16547   WALT DISNEY's STORY LAND

17865   A TREASURY OF DISNEY LITTLE
GOLDEN BOOKS

Walt Disney's
DUMBO
and the Magic Feather

A BOOK ABOUT CONFIDENCE

A GOLDEN BOOK • NEW YORK
Western Publishing Company, Inc., Racine, Wisconsin 53404

Once there was a baby circus elephant named Dumbo. Dumbo was soft and plump, with sparkling eyes. His legs were short and sturdy, and he had a little trunk. In fact, he was everything an elephant ought to be.

Now, all elephants have big ears, but Dumbo had ears that were huge! They made poor Dumbo the laughingstock of the circus.

Visitors to the big top made fun of Dumbo. "Get a load of them ears," one young bully sneered. "No wonder they call you Dumbo—you're the dumbest-lookin' animal I ever saw."

The other elephants weren't any kinder. They knew that every time Dumbo lined up at the end of their parade, he tripped over his own big ears. That made the spectators laugh and ruined the parade for the other elephants.

If it hadn't been for his one and only friend, Timothy
Mouse, Dumbo might have lost heart completely. Timothy
was very kind to Dumbo. He had all sorts of ideas about
making Dumbo a success.

Timothy thought Dumbo's big chance had come when the ringmaster started to train the baby elephant for a new act.

"We'll have all the elephants form a big pyramid," the ringmaster said. "Then Dumbo can spring from his springboard to the top and wave a flag!"

Dumbo tried and tried to do his trick right. "I'll never be able to do it," he thought. His ears kept getting in the way.

But Timothy had an idea. "We'll tie your ears up!" he said. "Then they can't get in the way."

Soon after, it was time for Dumbo to perform his new act in the center ring. He saw the big audience. He saw the other elephants. "They don't like me," he thought. "They don't want me in their act. I can't do this trick anyway."

As Dumbo ran to the springboard his ears came undone. He tripped and slid right into the elephant at the bottom of the pyramid. Crash! Bang! Down they all came. The act was ruined.

The ringmaster yelled at Dumbo. "You're a sorry excuse for an elephant. I'm through with you."

Then the clowns started to come up with ideas for Dumbo, but their ideas were mean. They wanted to make Dumbo a clown, so they set off firecrackers under his feet, threw pies in his face, and tripped him to make him look silly.

One day a clown came up with the cruelest plan of all.
"Let's dress Dumbo like a baby and make him jump off the
top floor of a burning building," he said.

"Wow!" another clown said.

"The audience will love it," said a third.

Poor Dumbo soon found himself trembling atop a fake burning building. Clowns dressed as firemen dashed around below. Then Dumbo felt a thwack on his back as one of the clowns sent him tumbling out a window. Head over heels, he crashed through a net and into a tub beneath it.

Time after time Dumbo had to do that act. But Timothy Mouse always helped the baby elephant clean himself up. He helped Dumbo cheer up, too.

"You're having a hard time," Timothy said. "But always do your best and believe in yourself, and you can do anything. You'll fly high!"

That night Dumbo had a dream. In the dream Dumbo was flapping his ears and flying. Timothy sat in the brim of Dumbo's cap. The dream seemed so real that Dumbo almost believed he *could* fly.

The next morning Dumbo and Timothy awoke with a
start. They saw blue sky above them and green grass far, far
below. They had spent the night in the branches of a very tall
tree. Nearby sat a flock of crows.

"How did we get up here?" Timothy asked.

"You must have flown," replied one of the crows.

"But we don't know how to fly," Timothy said.

"Nothing to it," the bird insisted. "All you do is flap your
wings, and up you go."

"We don't have wings," Timothy said.

"What about them?" asked a bird, pointing to Dumbo's ears.

"That's it, Dumbo!" Timothy cried. "You can fly! You'll be a star for sure!"

"Sure he can fly," said a crow. "It's easy as pie. But just for good measure"—he leaned over and handed Dumbo a shiny black feather—"take this. It's magic. We give them to all our young uns. Works every time. You never saw a crow that couldn't fly, now, did you?"

Dumbo clutched the magic feather in his trunk and
began to flap his ears. Dumbo flapped faster and faster, but
it was no use. He remained firmly on that big branch.

"You can do it, Dumbo," Timothy squeaked. "After all, you flew *up* here. I'm sure you can fly down." Timothy and the crows gave Dumbo a gentle push, and the little elephant was off the branch and up in the air.

At first Dumbo was so scared, he almost crashed. But then he remembered the magic feather. The feather made him feel that he could do anything. Swooping and swirling, gliding and whirling, Dumbo the elephant flew high in the sky!

At last Dumbo made a perfect landing. And then, after thanking the crows for their help, he took off again. With Timothy safe in the brim of his cap and the magic feather tight in his trunk, Dumbo headed happily back to the big top.

Dumbo got to the circus just in time for his act. He took his place on top of the burning building. As always, he waited till the flames had almost reached him before he jumped from the window.

But this time, instead of crashing through the net... Dumbo simply flapped his ears and gently glided off. Over the breathless audience he flew, around the astonished ringmaster, past the gaping clowns.

He was having so much fun that he completely forgot about the feather. Suddenly it slipped from his trunk and went floating down to the ground.

"Oh, no!" Dumbo thought. "I can't fly without it." And Dumbo began to fall.

With the crowd shrieking in alarm, Timothy had to
scream to be heard. "Come on, Dumbo, you can do it! You
don't need any feather to fly. All you need to do it is to
believe you can do it. Now flap those ears!"

Dumbo heard his friend. Spreading out his ears, he hovered just inches from the ground. He gave a little flutter, then a flap…and then he was flying higher than ever. The audience cheered as Dumbo the Flying Elephant stole the show.

When he landed, Dumbo hugged his friend Timothy in his trunk. "You see, Dumbo," Timothy said, "you *can* do anything, if you only believe you can."

Dumbo lived happily ever after as the star of the circus. People came from all over the world to see him fly. No one thought his ears were too big. In fact, the other elephants started trying to fly! But they never knew Dumbo's secret: He could do anything because he believed he could.